QUEST
for the EAGLE
FEATHER

by
JOHN DUNCKLEE

rising moon
Books for Young Readers from Northland Publishing

To my wife, Penny,

my children and grandchildren,

and Dick and Jean Wilson

The text type was set in Columbus
The display type was set in Celestia and Ovidius
Composed and manufactured in the United States of America
Designed by Mary C. Wages
Edited by Tom Carpenter
Production Supervised by Lisa Brownfield

FIRST IMPRESSION
ISBN 0-87358-668-9 (hc)
ISBN 0-87358-657-3 (sc)

Library of Congress Catalog Card Number pending

0601/2M/3-97 (hc)
0601/3.5/3-97 (sc)

Q UEST FOR THE EAGLE FEATHER is a work of fiction. The characters and narrative are from my imagination alone. It began as a bedtime story to my youngest son, Andy, when he was in the first grade. That particular bedtime came late because the story continued flowing from my storyteller mind. It was past midnight. Andy finally went to sleep. I went to my typewriter and spent the remainder of the night writing down the story.

I had just finished a three-year battle to save a sacred mountain from land developers. During that period, as a major segment of my research, I came to know the beauty of Native peoples' feelings for the sacred mountain. I have a continuing deep respect for Native people and their strong beliefs. This book is but one of my ways of showing that respect, not only toward all Native people, their cultures, and traditions, but also toward all sacred mountains.

I hope readers will find in *Quest for the Eagle Feather* an exciting story of adventure, acceptance, and growth told against the backdrop of multicultural traditions of family ties, spiritual connections with the natural world, and personal responsibility.

I

TALL DEER and Quiet Water walked from the cluster of rock dwellings in the small village to the far end of the mesa. Tall Deer had built a corral there many years before. The posts were juniper trunks with horizontal poles made from ash saplings. It was not a large enclosure, but big enough to hold ten horses. Neither Tall Deer, taller than other men of the Eagle Clan, nor Quiet Water, the blond and blue-eyed adopted son of Tall Deer, spoke as they walked along the narrow trail. A mouse-colored mare, with a white star on her forehead, and her black colt were the only animals inside the corral. As Tall Deer and Quiet Water approached, the mare shifted her hind legs to turn and watch them. The colt, suddenly robbed of his mother's milk, turned also. He bobbed his head up and down as he looked quizzically at Tall Deer and Quiet Water standing by the corral.

"He was born last night," Quiet Water announced. "I brought them in from the pasture by the river so you could see the colt."

"It is a good-looking colt," Tall Deer replied. "I am sure that you will do as well training him as you did his mother, White Star."

Quiet Water thought back to the day, three years before, when Tall Deer had given him the newborn filly to be trained. He also thought about the many hours he had spent on a ledge overlooking the river, wondering about his white parents. The idea of riding White Star to California in search of them dominated his thoughts.

"We must talk, my son," Tall Deer said, putting his right hand on Quiet Water's shoulder. "It has been seven winters since I found you and brought you to our home here on the mesa. I remember watching Blue-Flower-Blooming care for you until you came out of your sleep."

Quiet Water said, "The only thing I remember was riding on the back of the wagon while my father and mother were in front. A bolt of lightning spooked the team of horses, and they ran away, taking the wagon with them. A wheel must have hit a rock, because I felt myself flying through the air. The next thing I remember was Blue-Flower-Blooming smiling at me."

"She was very happy to see that you were alive."

"I was afraid. I didn't know where I was, or who you were."

"We knew that. We tried our best to give you love to drive away your fear. I rode out to the place in the broken country where I found you to see if I could find your father and mother, but they were long gone in the direction of the setting sun."

"They were going to California to look for gold."

"You have learned much since you came to live in the village. It was not long until you began to speak our language, and you made friends with Running Fox and Screaming Crow."

Quiet Water laughed as he recalled the time he ran away to find his mother and father.

"What is making you laugh, my son?" Tall Deer asked.

"I am thinking about the time I went away to find my white parents. When you found me by Water-from-the-Rocks, I was asleep and hungry. I watched how you made the fire with your fire tools. I was very happy to see you."

"Blue-Flower-Blooming and I have come to love you as our own son. We still have that love for you."

A few moments of silence passed between the two. Quiet Water knew how much his Indian parents loved him. He also loved them, but the idea of finding his white parents was as strong as ever.

"It is time for you to learn more," Tall Deer said. "Swift Elk is waiting to talk to you and your two friends about your coming-of-age ceremony."

"I must open the gate in the corral so White Star and her colt can go out to graze," Quiet Water said.

As he walked around the corral toward the gate, the blond-haired boy, dressed in buckskin leggings and moccasins and his buckskin shirt, felt like making some excuse not to go to the house of the old medicine man, Swift Elk. He knew of the coming-of-age ceremony, and he didn't want to participate in it until he was sure he belonged with the Eagle Clan.

After opening the gate, he tried to think of some excuse, but nothing came to his mind. He returned to Tall Deer's side, and the two walked along the narrow streets between the rock houses of the village. As they approached the medicine man's house, Tall Deer stopped, turning toward Quiet Water.

"This is between you and your companions and Swift Elk. The medicine man is very wise, and you will learn much from him. I must leave you now, my son."

Tall Deer placed his right hand on the boy's shoulder for a moment, then turned, and walked to the rock house he shared with Blue-Flower-Blooming and his blond-haired adopted son.

Quiet Water hesitated before joining Running Fox and Screaming Crow seated in front of the old medicine man. He wanted to run somewhere and hide. But that would hurt Tall Deer and Blue-Flower-Blooming. He didn't want that to happen. Joining his friends, Quiet Water sat down beside them, facing Swift Elk.

2

CHAPTER TWO

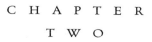

IT IS THAT TIME in your lives when you must prepare yourselves to climb the Sacred Mountain to watch the eagle fly," the old medicine man said. The three young boys sat cross-legged and silent in front of him. His aged, cloudy eyes sparkled suddenly as he spoke. The boys looked directly at the old man's dark face grooved by eighty years in the weather of the four seasons, and the steel gray hair held in place by a scarlet headband. The important moment had arrived; the old medicine man's instructions for their coming-into-manhood journey to the Sacred Mountain.

"Look at her," the old man said, pointing to the distant mountain rising abruptly from the surrounding plateau. "So majestic, so beautiful; she is the home of our gods."

The three boys had looked at the Sacred Mountain every day, but now the peaks seemed higher and more mysterious than before. Their eyes returned to the old man as he continued. "You each must make a new bow and twelve arrows for your journey," he said. "Hunting is different on the Sacred Mountain. The game is fast, and there are many tall trees."

The boys had made many bows and arrows during the years they learned to hunt, but the new bows would have to be stronger and heavier to send the arrows at the greatest speeds possible. They would be depending completely on their weapons for food and protection during their stay on the slopes of the Sacred Mountain.

"You will begin your journey before the summer rains begin," the old medicine man continued. "Your approach will be from the direction of the rising sun, and before you reach the steep slopes leading to the summit you will see a grassy meadow in the middle of a long valley. Here you will make your camp for sleeping and eating. It is forbidden to sleep or camp higher, where the rain god stays. Each day you must climb the tallest peak and wait for the eagle to appear."

Until this point in the instructions, the old man spoke to the three boys as one. Now, he spoke to them individually.

"Running Fox, you are the fleet one. You have won all the foot races in our village, but speed alone will not be enough. You will need strength to climb the steep slopes that will rob your lungs of breath."

The shortest of the three boys squirmed in his cross-legged position.

"Above all, you must learn patience, something the swift rarely have."

Running Fox was proud of his ability to run fast. He wondered how the old man knew of his impatience. He wanted to ask, but kept silent, according to tradition, as the old man gave instructions. Running Fox was not only the shortest of the three, he was also the stockiest. His face was rounder, and his eyes looked like narrow slits under his unusually thick, bushy eyebrows. Like the others, his hair hung below his shoulders. But Running Fox's hair was bluish-black with a natural wave to it that his father said came from the time of deep sickness when Running Fox's body felt like it burned.

The medicine man turned slowly to look at the next boy. "Screaming Crow, you are the hunter. You are the best at hiding your trail, especially when you hide from the work in the fields, but know this: You can hide nothing on the Sacred Mountain."

Screaming Crow, a tall youth with large eyes set in perfect proportion to his thin, angular face, blushed at the medicine man's words. It was true that he loved to hunt and that he often hid from all the boring work in the fields.

Swift Elk turned to Quiet Water. He didn't speak for a few moments, as if he was deciding what to say to the young man with the piercing blue eyes and a mouth set in a manner that suggested stubborn determination.

The medicine man spoke slowly, choosing his words carefully. "You have not always been with us. In the seven winters you have been in our village, you have become like a son to Tall Deer and Blue-Flower-Blooming, and now it is time for a boy your age to undertake the quest for the eagle feather."

"There are those among the elders who think you are not a member of the Eagle Clan. There are those who think you are not worthy of this quest." Swift Elk looked closely at Quiet Water. "If they are correct and you leave us, you put the Eagle Clan at great risk. Our rituals are not meant to be shared with others. To do so will anger our spirits and bring great misfortune down upon our village."

Quiet Water said, "I would never—"

"It is not your place to speak," said Swift Elk. "I agreed with the elders who doubted you, until I heard Tall Deer speak on your behalf. He said that only the quest for the eagle feather will answer our doubts." Again, he looked closely at Quiet Water. "And yours."

Swift Elk rose to his feet. "When you three return from your journey to the Sacred Mountain, I will be here to greet you and to receive a feather from the eagle as a gift to his Clan."

3

CHAPTER THREE

T HE BOYS WALKED along the pathways between the stone houses after the old medicine man dismissed them. They came to the narrow trail that led to the valley floor beneath the mesa. Below, as they approached the river, Running Fox broke the silence. "We must search for the strongest ash saplings for our new bows," he said.

"Black Canyon has the best obsidian for our arrowheads," Screaming Crow added.

Quiet Water was silent. He thought about what the old medicine man had said about the elders being concerned that he might betray the secrets of the eagle clan. He felt hurt that there were those who did not trust him. But he remembered the many hours he had spent on the ledge wondering about his real parents. Had they reached California? Would they ever return for him?

The two Indian boys had always respected their friend's desire to be alone. "Quiet Water is sitting on his ledge today," Running Fox might say. "Maybe he will join us down by the river when he is finished with his thinking."

Or, it would be Screaming Crow. "Quiet Water does not tell us what he thinks about on his ledge, but I have an idea what it is."

The two friends never asked Quiet Water about his time on the ledge, just as now, while the three walked down the narrow trail toward the river, they respected the silence of their clan brother.

Quiet Water knew he must decide whether to stay with the Eagle Clan or leave and try to find the life that the thunderstorm had taken from him. If he chose to remain as a member of the Eagle Clan, there would always be the distrust of those who feared that he would someday betray their secrets. Somehow, Quiet Water knew he must gain the trust of the elders if he was to continue to live in the village of stone houses on top of the mesa. "I don't know what to do. Maybe

I'll find the answer on the Sacred Mountain." He nodded to himself. "I will show them. I will go to the Sacred Mountain. I will stay there until I see the eagle fly."

Quiet Water dismissed his thoughts as they slowly approached the river. "Screaming Crow, Running Fox," he said. "It was just two sunrises ago that I saw some ash saplings along the river where it makes the big bend. They looked perfect for our new bows and arrows. Follow me; I will show them to you."

As they walked, they talked about new bows and arrows. Screaming Crow changed the subject abruptly.

"We are the best of friends and like brothers in the Eagle Clan," he said. "I want to talk about this journey to the Sacred Mountain and the instructions of Swift Elk. Before we cut the ash saplings for our new bows, we need to share what is in our hearts."

They stopped and sat beneath the broad canopy of a tall Cottonwood tree.

"Swift Elk has said that there are those of our clan who doubt Quiet Water," Screaming Crow said. "It's strange to me that anyone would fear that Quiet Water would betray our clan to strangers." He swept his hand from his chest toward his friends. "We are the same age and we've grown up together like brothers. I've seen you on your ledge staring off into the distance. I know that it is good to be alone sometimes."

Screaming Crow picked up a stone and threw it. "The Elders don't know you like we do," he said. "If you decide to leave our clan, I will be the first to offer you my strongest bow for your journey. I know the secrets of the Eagle Clan will always be safe with you."

Running Fox spoke. "Quiet Water, you have been our brother during our years of learning. You have never betrayed us in any manner. I, too, know that you would not betray the secrets of the Eagle Clan, even if you should someday decide to leave us to find your other people. I would be sad to say farewell to you. You are as Indian as we are. There are only the differences of our hair and skin, and that is not reason to distrust you, clan brother."

Screaming Crow began to speak, but Running Fox held up his hand to show that he had not yet finished. After a moment, he continued.

"Quiet Water, even though I trust you with my life, I also respect our elders. I can see why they would have their doubts, but I am not asking you to tell me what it is you think about sitting on your ledge. Those thoughts are your thoughts. You must struggle with yours just as we must struggle with ours. There. I have told you what is in my heart. I do not hesitate to begin this journey to the Sacred Mountain with you."

The three fell silent for a few moments. Then Quiet Water spoke softly. "Running Fox and Screaming Crow, you have shown me that you are my brothers in many ways. Perhaps in more ways than I've shown to you. I don't know what the next sunrise will bring, but you both will always be my brothers. The burden I bear is mine alone. I hope I will find an answer on the Sacred Mountain."

He rose to his feet. "Let's speak no more of it."

The three young initiates walked to the bend in the river near Painted Cliffs where they found the grove of ash saplings. The trees were a perfect age for strong, resilient bows. When seasoned properly, their bows would send arrows swiftly to their targets. There was also a bounty of smaller trees that would provide straight, strong arrows. Each selected the trees he wanted for his new weapons.

The youths worked for two days, shaping and lashing

them onto a framework designed to retain the shape of the bows while they seasoned. An extra "pilot" bow, lashed next to the others, would serve as a test when the boys felt their bows were ready for stringing. They made the overnight trip to the Black Canyon in search of the finest obsidian for the tips of their arrows.

4

C H A P T E R

F O U R

THE FIRST high summer clouds began drifting in slowly during their return trip to the village. The boys spent their long summer days carrying water to the hills of corn, beans, and pumpkins.

When small ears began poking their way out on the stalks of corn, the boys decided to test the pilot bow that would tell them whether their bows were ready. They walked to the framework where the new bows remained lashed. "I hope it tells us good news," Screaming Crow said. "I am anxious to leave for the scared mountain to watch the eagle fly."

Quiet Water said nothing as he turned to gaze at the peaks of the Sacred Mountain shrouded in clouds.

He too hoped that they could start soon. To ease the fears of the elders, he had stopped spending time on the ledge. Instead, he spent sleepless nights along the river where he watched the moonlight reflect on the rippling water of the stream. He struggled with his two identities. During the day he was Quiet Water, adopted son of Tall Deer and Blue-Flower-Blooming of the Eagle Clan. When the bright stars appeared and slowly wheeled around the night sky, Quiet Water became John Butler and John Butler became Quiet Water again and again, until the rising sun once more revealed the Sacred Mountain.

The boys reached the framework, and Screaming Crow unlashed the pilot shaft. He took it to where two juniper trees grew close together, and placed the shaft between the trunks. They took turns trying to break the shaft, but it held its strength and shape. The boys smiled at one another.

Quiet Water was first to unlash his new bow from the framework. He ran his hands over the curvature of the strong ash bow that was ready for stringing with the twisted gut of a bobcat.

They fitted obsidian points into the ends of the

arrow shafts, wrapped them with sinew, and applied pine pitch to keep the sinew from unraveling. Then came the feathers, which had to be attached accurately to the other ends of the shafts with more pitch. Finally, the bows and arrows were finished, and they were ready to leave on their journey.

Quiet Water said good-bye to Tall Deer and Blue-Flower-Blooming. She briefly held his face in her cool hands, looking at him with moist eyes and a smile, then she turned and entered their house. Although Tall Deer had been concerned about Quiet Water's sleepless nights beside the river, he felt great pride in his adopted son. Tall Deer placed one hand on Quiet Water's shoulder. With his other hand, he presented Quiet Water with a silver bracelet.

"Wear this to the Sacred Mountain to watch the eagle fly," Tall Deer said. "This bracelet will bring you safely home to your mother and father."

Quiet Water slipped the bracelet onto his wrist, admiring it. "Do not fear for me, Father," he said. "I will return unless there is no life in my body."

"There is something else I want you to take with you to the Sacred Mountain," Tall Deer said. He handed Quiet Water a narrow quiver containing a single arrow. "This is a special arrow in its own special quiver. It was passed down to me by my father, who received it from his father. It was made before he was born. The arrow was used only once that I know. My father's father sent it into the heart of a cougar that had sprung from a tree branch, and was hurtling toward him. If not for this special arrow, my father's father would have been killed by the cougar. There is also a story about it being used when the men in metal hats and shirts came. The special arrow is said to have helped send them away."

Quiet Water took the special arrow from the narrow quiver, looked at it carefully, and felt the smooth, straight shaft with his thumb and forefinger. "The feathers are from the eagle, but what wood is the shaft?"

"The shaft wood is from a tree that grows in the dry lands. The grain is long and has great strength. It is said that the tree has spines on its branches that are like the claws of the cat with the short tail."

"The arrow point is not from Black Canyon," Quiet Water said. "It is white."

Tall Deer nodded. "I was told that the arrow point came from a distant land brought by a trader. It is not known when nor who made the arrow point. The important thing to remember is that the special arrow should be used when you must defend your life against the threat of an attacking animal or, if the case may be, another man."

"How will I know when I must use this arrow and not those I have made?" Quiet Water asked.

"Somehow," Tall Deer said. "The special arrow will find its way to your bow."

The boys set off in the cool morning air toward the majestic Sacred Mountain through the miles of sage-brush clumps with yellow, straw-colored grasses in between. When the sun stood in the middle of the sky, they reached the point where juniper trees grew along the banks of arroyos. The heat of the summer sun slowed their pace.

They rested in the shade of a large juniper tree. Quiet Water thought about his mouse-colored mare and her black colt grazing in the pasture near the village on the mesa. If he decided to leave his life with the Indians, White Star could carry him to California to search for his white parents. Where were they? Were they alive?

Running Fox, impatient to continue the journey, rose to his feet. "We should keep going," he said.

"Our horses would make this trip much easier," Quiet Water said.

"I agree," Screaming Crow said. "But, according to my father, this journey to the Sacred Mountain is a tradition that began before the men wearing metal hats and shirts brought horses to the land. That is why we cannot ride our horses to the Sacred Mountain."

Quiet Water and Screaming Crow stood up, and the three travelers resumed their pace toward the mountain on the distant horizon. As they walked along, Running Fox asked Quiet Water how he had learned about training horses. Running Fox and Screaming Crow respected their blond-haired friend for his way with his filly.

"Before I came to the village, I was always around horses. I watched my white father break and train young horses."

"When we race our horses along the river, you always come first," Screaming Crow remarked.

"It is White Star who wins the races, not me," Quiet Water replied.

"But you trained her," Screaming Crow insisted. "Will you show me how you train horses?"

"When we return from the mountain, you may watch me working with White Star's black colt."

As the boys trudged through the bunch grass, the heat from the sun grew more intense. In the afternoon light, the Sacred Mountain seemed farther away than ever.

5

JUST BEFORE SUNSET the three approached a large river of muddy, red water that spilled over a red sandstone cliff, forming a large waterfall. Beyond the plunging cascade, a still pool of brown water seemed to be waiting for its turn to continue downstream.

The boys stripped off their deerskin leggings, shirts, and moccasins, eager to cool themselves in the large pool. "You are as pale as a yellow beaver, Quiet Water," Running Fox said, splashing his friend.

"Ha, Running Fox," Quiet Water said. "You and Screaming Crow are the color of the muddy water in this pool just like the turtles you are! The yellow beaver will beat the two brown turtles to the other side of the pool." They raced across the pool. At the far side, they splashed and tussled until exhaustion forced them to climb onto the river bank. The sun sank below the horizon in a blaze of color, filling the sky and bouncing off the evening clouds until darkness invaded the desert of the vast and silent plateau. Sleep came easily after the long trek the boys made on their first day of the journey to the Sacred Mountain.

Quiet Water was first to open his eyes as morning arrived with the first glimmer of light over the land. He sat up and looked over at his sleeping friends. He thought about the fun they had had racing in the pool the previous evening. Then his thoughts darted back to swimming in the river near the farm in Tennessee when he was John Butler. Even if he should leave his life on the mesa, he wouldn't find his real parents in Tennessee because they were in California, unless . . .

"Hoopa, you two lazy ones. Let us be on our way, if we are to reach the meadow in the long valley by nightfall. Or will it take two days for the turtles to get there? Get up! The first to shoot a rabbit has the choice of the tastiest part."

Screaming Crow and Running Fox pulled on their leggings, grabbed their bows and arrows, and followed

Quiet Water into the brush to look for a breakfast of small game. A cottontail rabbit dashed from a clump of sagebrush, and before Screaming Crow and Quiet Water could get arrows from their quivers, Running Fox sent an arrow straight through the rabbit's heart. As Running Fox ran to claim his prey, Quiet Water saw another jump from its hiding place, and quickly had his breakfast.

Running Fox could not resist the opportunity to make fun of Screaming Crow. "Screaming Crow, we will not let you start the day hungry. Quiet Water and I will give you the tails from our rabbits!"

"That will be fine, my brother," Screaming Crow said. "When I shoot the first deer, I will give the hooves and the antlers to you and Quiet Water!"

Once on the trail, their foolishness changed to determination. Eagerly, they pushed on, especially Running Fox, who showed his impatience by setting a pace the others found difficult to maintain. At a resting point Screaming Crow walked over to a piñon tree to examine the cones. "This will be a good year for piñon nuts," he said. "These cones are full."

Near the base of the mountain, the trees changed from scrubby piñon and juniper to stately pines, some more than a hundred feet tall. The reddish-orange trunks, bare of lower branches, reached toward the sky with branches adorned by long, green needles. Dry, straw-colored grass carpeted the forest floor. Young, tender, green shoots sprouted, using what remained of the moisture from the melted winter snow.

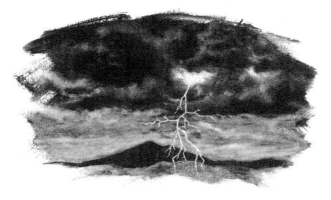

White thunderheads flew much closer to the land than during the days before. The clouds slowed and came together, billowing, boiling, and darkening into a swelling storm. The boys sought shelter beneath a giant Ponderosa pine. A lightning bolt streaked earthward, and moments later an ear-splitting crack of thunder shook the ground.

The dry storm rushed closer, still just lightning and thunder. Rain had not started to fall from the giant, black cloud. Suddenly, a lightning bolt lit up the forest with the loud blast of thunder: cracking at the same time. A tall, standing dead pine exploded and burst into flame, scattering a shower of burning pieces onto the grass-covered floor of the forest. The wind fanned a grass fire that wound its way among the trees, blackening the lower trunks, but never reaching the needle-laden limbs. The three boys watched speechless from their position upwind from the fire. The flames consumed the dried grasses and low-growing gooseberry bushes. Red and orange embers of deadfall branches flickered with fingers of fire among the blackened ashes of the charred ground. The fire burned the forest floor clean of dead grass and fallen needles that had accumulated for several years, since lightning had last started a fire in the area.

The first drops of rain sizzled into steam as they hit the embers. The storm cloud began to empty its load of moisture onto the forest in sheets of pelting rain. A wall of water seemed to pour down all at once. The boys lost sight of the fire and the forest, except for nearby trunks, and shivered in their rain-soaked buckskin shirts and leggings, in spite of the sheltering canopy of the tall pines.

The storm moved on, thundering in the distance, leaving the trees dripping droplets from their dark green needles and cones. The sun returned, turning the wet bark and needles into a glistening spectacle. "That was quite a storm," Screaming Crow said, impressed.

"The lightning and thunder scared me for a while," Quiet Water said. "It was too close, and reminded me of another storm."

"We should get started again," Running Fox said. "The storm has delayed us long enough."

"It might be better to make our camp here for the night, and start out again when the sun rises," Screaming Crow suggested.

"Everything is soaking wet here," Running Fox said, anxious to reach their destination.

"The sun will dry us before darkness comes," Quiet Water said. "I would like to stay here, then begin walking as the first light of the sun arrives. Besides, we should hunt for food."

"I think Quiet Water speaks well," Screaming Crow said. "We must not be impatient to reach the Sacred Mountain when we should hunt. Besides, I am getting hungry."

"Then let us hunt first," Running Fox said. "We can camp when we have found food."

They walked along the edge of the scorched ground

and saw the green shoots of grasses between the charred, blackened stalks that had been yellowish-brown before the fire. The scents of smoke and rain-freshened air mingled.

Running Fox, as usual, took the lead. They walked slowly, searching for game. Running Fox stopped short, and slowly lowered himself to the ground. The other two boys did the same, until they too were stretched on the ground. They crawled slowly, using their elbows, to where Running Fox waited.

"There's a small herd of antelope ahead," Running Fox whispered. "Let's crawl to that large boulder up ahead where we can stay hidden. Screaming Crow, you go first. We will follow."

The antelope were so intent on nibbling at the tender, green, grass shoots exposed by the fire that they didn't notice the three boys squirming along the ground on their bellies toward the large, blackish boulder.

"Quiet Water," Screaming Crow whispered, when all three crouched at the side of the boulder away from the grazing antelope. "Put your headband on an arrow. Lift it just over the top of the boulder, and wave it slowly. Antelope are curious. Maybe they will walk over to see what is happening, and come within the range of our bows. Running Fox and I will stay hidden until we have a shot."

Quiet Water tied his red headband around an arrow, raised it above the boulder, and waved it slowly, back and forth. The other two boys waited on their bellies, flattened against the moist, blackened ground.

When it was obvious that the antelope were not going to look up from their feast, Screaming Crow gave out the sound of a crow calling to its mate. The antelope stopped nibbling at the grass shoots and raised their heads in the direction of the boulder. Quiet Water continued to wave his red headband. A doe and yearling started toward the motion of the headband first. The others began to follow, cautiously, wondering what was moving over the top of the boulder.

Running Fox and Screaming Crow hugged the ground, each peeking around his end of the boulder with arrows set in their bowstrings, ready to draw back and send the arrows into their prey. They waited. Quiet Water changed hands on the shaft of the arrow without stopping the waving. He wanted to see the antelope.

Screaming Crow watched as the doe and yearling

31

advanced, little by little, toward him. Finally, when they were within range of his bow, he pulled the bowstring back with all the strength in his arms. He wanted the yearling. Slowly, he walked on his knees around the end of the boulder. The doe saw him and jumped but the yearling stood still, watching the moving headband.

Screaming Crow's arrow flew swiftly to its mark behind the yearling's foreleg. The yearling jumped, took a few steps, and toppled over. The arrow from Running Fox's bow was too late, and plummeted into the ground.

"Hoopa!" Screaming Crow yelled to his friends. "I have our supper. You two may have the antlers and the hooves!"

Quiet Water stopped waving the headband on his arrow, and stood up. The rest of the herd scampered off and disappeared into the forest.

They made their camp for the night. Quiet Water prepared the meat for cooking and Running Fox went to the unburned area of the forest to gather dead wood for their fire. Screaming Crow sat with his back against a tree, repairing the arrow he had retrieved from the antelope.

Running Fox carried four heavy armloads of dead

branches and stacked them next to the boulder. He opened the deerskin pouch in which he carried live coals from the morning fire. "The fire pouch is soaking wet," he said, looking inside at the dead, black chunks of what were once hot coals.

"We can look for something that might still be burning from the fire," Quiet Water suggested.

"You go look for coals while I go out to gather some dried grass," Running Fox said. "How are you doing with the antelope, Screaming Crow?"

"I will be finished soon," Screaming Crow said.

Quiet Water took his fire tools from his pouch. The shredded cedar bark was damp from the rain, so he placed it in the sunlight on the boulder. "My tinder is too wet to light with the fire tools," he told Screaming Crow. "Maybe there is enough sun left to dry it."

Running Fox gathered a bunch of dead grass stalks.

"The grass is still damp from the rain, but it might dry enough in the sun that is left," he said, and scattered the grass next to the cedar bark. Quiet Water and Running Fox went over to help Screaming Crow as they waited for the shredded cedar bark and grass to dry in the afternoon sun.

The sun had begun to disappear behind the mountain when they decided to attempt making a fire. Quiet Water felt the shredded cedar bark to see if it was dry enough. "I hope this will make fire," he said. "I don't like eating raw meat."

He gathered his fire tools: a small bow strung with a deerskin thong; a straight, pointed stick that fit into a beveled hole in a flat, thin piece of wood; and a flat, oval, palm-sized stone with an indentation worn in the center. Beneath the wood with the beveled hole, he placed a small amount of shredded cedar bark. He then placed the pointed stick into the hole and took one turn with the thong on the bow around the pointed stick. With his left hand he placed the stone over the rounded top of the pointed stick, and with his right he began the back and forth motion with the bow to turn the pointed stick in the beveled hole. This created friction and heat. Briskly and patiently, Quiet Water moved the bow back and forth the way he had seen Tall Deer do it so many times before.

6

C H A P T E R

S I X

THE CEDAR BARK finally began smoking. When he was sure there were enough coals in the bark, Quiet Water dropped the tools, took the smoldering bark in his cupped hands, and blew gently into it until the bark burst into a small flame.

Running Fox placed some small twigs in a pile, ready for the fire. Quiet Water slipped the burning bark beneath the twigs, and soon there was a crackling fire next to the boulder. The boys rested quietly as the fire burned down to coals. Quiet Water laid strips of meat on them to roast. When they finished eating, they divided the rest and put the chunks into their hunting bags. Then they placed more wood on the fire.

Quiet Water took the first watch for cougars or bear that might smell the freshly killed antelope and come around to investigate. He also kept fuel on the fire. Running Fox took the second turn, Screaming Crow the last until sunrise.

The night was clear and a half-moon gave a little light for a while, until it disappeared behind the Sacred Mountain. Nothing invaded their camp and when the sun peeked brightly over the horizon, Screaming Crow let the fire turn again to coals and roasted more of the meat, and the liver and heart. After a sumptuous morning meal, the three boys packed up and headed for the Sacred Mountain's interior valley. In the distance they saw deer and antelope foraging on the tender leaves of the grasses pushing through the ashes of the fire. The sky began to fill with flying clouds, bringing moisture to be released somewhere on the land. The boys concentrated on reaching the valley described by the old medicine man. Running Fox, in the lead, set a fast walking pace for the other two. He was impatient to arrive at their destination.

The slope of the land became steeper, and Running

Fox had to slow his pace as they climbed toward the long valley, hidden by the Sacred Mountain. They stopped to rest near a cliff from which they could look out and see where they had been traveling.

"I can almost see our mesa from here," Screaming Crow said.

"The Sacred Mountain is much farther than it looked from our village."

"Let's keep going," Running Fox said impatiently. "I am anxious to find the long valley. We are on the Sacred Mountain now, and it makes no difference where our mesa is until we have seen the eagle fly."

"Running Fox is in such a hurry," Screaming Crow said to Quiet Water. "Could it be that he is impatient to be looking at the moon again with the pretty girl from the Bear Clan?"

Quiet Water laughed, but color rushed into Running Fox's face. He was not ashamed of his feelings for the girl from the Bear Clan, but he was embarrassed that his two companions had seen through his impatience.

As they climbed higher, clumps of oak grew here and there among the ponderosa and another pine with shorter needles and different colored bark. There were also large groves of white-barked aspen with their broad, green leaves that seemed to sing in the wind.

A group of deer bounded out of their way, but the boys did not attempt to use their bows. The meat in their hunting bags would fill their needs for a while. The climb up the mountain was difficult enough without being burdened by a deer carcass.

Suddenly, a family of wild turkeys, frightened by the presence of the boys, took flight with a loud whirring sound from their large, swiftly flapping wings. The three stopped to watch the birds disappear among the trees. "Turkeys seem to come out of nowhere," Screaming Crow said. "We never would have had a shot at them."

"We are walking, not hunting," Running Fox replied.

"We may still get a chance to hunt the turkeys," Quiet Water said. "If we're on the mountain long enough."

"It will not take long for us to watch the eagle fly," Running Fox said.

"You think too much about the pretty girl from the Bear Clan," Screaming Crow said, and laughed.

"You think only about riding your horse and hunting," Running Fox replied. "If you find a pretty girl to think about, you will learn that it is nice to think about a pretty girl."

"Maybe you are right," Screaming Crow said. "But, you seem to have no other thoughts except for that pretty girl."

Quiet Water listened to his two friends harass each other. Finally, he started climbing the mountain slope. Running Fox and Screaming Crow followed.

More huge, white thunderheads filled the sky and flew faster than the boys had ever seen. Everything looked strange to them. They walked in a different world with the feeling they were entering a village of strangers for the first time.

They followed a small mountain stream. The trees grew closer together, and as they climbed higher they saw a different kind of tree with a blue tinge to its needles. Further up, where the forest opened, a shorter pine with short needles and bristly cones on its branches grew. There were groves of white-barked aspen of different heights with leaves fluttering in the wind, breaking the near-silence of the forest. Quiet Water thought about the silence as they rested. He listened to bird calls, to the wind, to the aspen leaves, and to a low, almost imperceptible hum. Trees, grass, and shrubs were growing. Insects were carrying on their lives. There was too much life on the mountain for absolute silence.

Running Fox was the first to stand and continue the climb up the steep mountainside, following a game trail.

Suddenly, as they came around a large aspen grove, the forest gave way to a spacious meadow filled with brightly blooming flowers of reds, pinks, yellows, and several shades of blue and purple, all bending gracefully in the mountain breeze. The boys stopped in their tracks to gaze at the beautiful meadow. A few deer and elk lifted their heads from grazing as the strange scent of the boys reached their nostrils.

"This must be where Swift Elk told us to make our camp," Running Fox said.

"Look," Quiet Water said, pointing. "That must be the peak."

The deer and elk glided gracefully into the large aspen grove in the middle of the meadow. Thunderheads moved closer and blackened, and thunder echoed through the valley. The boys hastened into the shelter of the aspen grove as the storm drenched the grasses and flowers in the meadow. "It appears the rain god welcomes us," Screaming Crow said.

"Perhaps we should make our camp here in the shelter of these trees," Running Fox suggested.

"I think we should wait here for the end of the rain god's welcome," Quiet Water said. "Then we can find a place closer to the base of the highest peak."

For the first time since the journey began, Running Fox forgot his impatience as he watched the storm, and thought about the climb they would have to make to reach the top of the highest peak of the Sacred Mountain.

The rain stopped as suddenly as it had begun and the boys left the aspen grove to find a camping place near the base of the tallest peak. The peak loomed far above, ominous and challenging.

"Look at the steepness of the slope, my brothers," Screaming Crow said. "We must find the best route for our climb to the top, or we will spend all our days going up instead of waiting for the eagle to fly."

7

C H A P T E R

S E V E N

THE SACRED MOUNTAIN had once been a fiery volcano, and had stood higher, before the rains and winds had washed and blown at the rocky summit, filling the crater with soil from the slopes above. Life in the meadow thrived in the rich, volcanic soil. Ridges of rock interrupted the slopes, where lava had cooled quickly and hardened during the eruption. The lava from the volcano had covered all the ground, but through time the rains had washed away the softer material leaving the ridges exposed. One of those ridges began near the summit, and continued down almost to the meadow.

"Look!" Quiet Water said. "There is a ridge that goes

almost to the top of the peak. A perfect way for our climb."

"It looks difficult," Screaming Crow said. "But it is the most direct way to the top."

Screaming Crow walked quietly away from his companions and entered the aspen grove. He had spotted a young buck deer and decided to stalk him. The buck had never seen humans before and watched curiously. Screaming Crow stopped behind one of the large aspen trees to wait for the deer to turn its head. The young buck lost his curiosity, and began to strip the tender aspen leaves from a young tree. Screaming Crow advanced to another large trunk. The deer concentrated on his meal. When he was within twenty paces of the buck, Screaming Crow showed himself to

the deer. The young buck scampered away, snapping dead branches on the ground as he went. Screaming Crow, the hunter, smiled as he watched the buck's white tail disappear among the aspen trees. They still had plenty of antelope meat.

Running Fox and Screaming Crow went in search of the spring that Swift Elk had told them about, leaving Quiet Water to start the fire. They followed a game trail through the meadow to the far side, where they saw a long swath of young trees snapped off at their bases lying dead on the slope. "Swift Elk didn't mention this," Running Fox said.

"These dead trees look like they were trampled down," Screaming Crow said. "Snow must have slid off the mountain peaks all at once."

"You are probably right, my brother," Running Fox said. "Look up on the mountain. There is a path with no trees all the way up."

"These trees will make a good frame for a lean-to," Screaming Crow suggested. "We can break off the dead branches and carry enough back to our camp."

They had carried the trees a short distance when they heard the sound of gurgling water. A spring with clear, cold water spilled from between some lava boulders. The boys looked carefully at the surrounding ground for tracks of animals using the spring.

"Look here," Screaming Crow said. "Here's a cougar's paw marks, and over there I see a bear's long footprint."

"There's a lot of deer and elk sign, too," Running Fox said.

They drank their fill of the refreshing mountain spring water. After filling their water bags made from the bladders of peccary, the wild piglike animals that provided strong-tasting meat, they returned to the place they had chosen for their camp. Quiet Water had not only started their fire, but was roasting the foreleg of the antelope. "We saw bear and cougar sign by the spring," Screaming Crow said to Quiet Water. "We also found these trees to use as a frame for a lean-to."

"When we have finished eating and building the lean-to, we'll need to gather enough wood to make certain the fire will last until morning."

The evening meal of roasted antelope satisfied the boys. Screaming Crow began building the lean-to as the others went into the aspen grove to gather deadfalls. He cut thongs from the antelope hide to lash the poles together for the frame. Then he lashed on more poles to the frame for rafters. The young aspen saplings and tall grasses furnished the material to thatch the roof.

Running Fox took Quiet Water to the snow slide where they gathered several more dead trees and dragged them back to camp. When they had enough firewood for the night, Quiet Water and Running Fox thatched the roof of the lean-to.

"I hope this will shed the raindrops when the rain god decides to return to this meadow," Screaming Crow said from where he stood in the shade of a tall pine.

They took turns again keeping the fire going and watching for any intruding cougar or bear that might decide to visit their camp. The Sacred Mountain reflected the moonlight into the old crater, giving the slopes and peaks an eerie look that all three noticed. They heard a wolf howling in the distance. The lonely cry filled the meadow. Another howl answered the first. Soon the howling stopped and the three clan brothers finished their final preparations for night.

8

CHAPTER EIGHT

QUIET WATER took the first turn at the fire. While his friends slept, he thought about the mountains near the home he left in Tennessee. He compared them with the Sacred Mountain: the differences in height, ruggedness, and grandeur. It was not Tennessee that he missed. There, he would never have been sent out to climb those mountains to watch the eagle fly. He might never have learned to hunt antelope, deer, and elk in Tennessee. He had learned about horses on the farm. For that he was glad, because his two friends respected his knowledge. White Star was one of the best horses in the village on the mesa. He remembered the happiness he felt when Tall Deer had told him how proud he was of his blond-haired son.

Quiet Water looked up at the tallest peak on the Sacred Mountain. It was bathed in the moonlight. He wondered how many days of climbing they would have to do before the eagle arrived for them to watch. Time did not matter like it did back on the farm in Tennessee, when his father had told him to hurry and get the corn field planted, or to work late to get the hay stacked before a rain.

He tried to imagine what life would be like in California, looking for gold. His father was probably in a hurry there, too. But here on the Sacred Mountain, there seemed to be no time, just the rising and setting of the sun, the glow of the moon, and the peaceful-ness of all the life around. Only Running Fox was in a hurry to return to the pretty girl from the Bear Clan. Quiet Water suddenly realized that, although it might seem there was no time on the Sacred Mountain or back in the village on the mesa, it was just a different kind of time. A different time for different people, and he was becoming less different from the people on the mesa the more time passed.

He felt himself getting sleepy, and tossed more wood on the fire before waking Screaming Crow for his turn as firetender and lookout.

The coals of the fire were ready for cooking their breakfast. It was during the last moments of darkness just before dawn, when Running Fox roused his companions. They cooked more of the antelope as they watched the fire without speaking, each with thoughts about the coming climb to wait for the eagle.

Daylight oozed into the old crater, slowly burning away the mist of the early, mountain morning. The boys looked up to their summit goal as they climbed toward the ridge. The lofty peak glittered in the gold sunrise while the valley below remained in murky, half darkness. The higher they climbed, the shorter the trees became, until there were only small, scattered trees lying nearly flat as if they were asleep. Beyond the last tree, tiny flowers grew in patches of soil that had collected between some of the boulders. The yellow, pink, and purple flowers gave life to the otherwise stark, boulder-strewn landscape above treeline.

The boys gasped for breath and their legs ached when they reached the rocky summit of the Sacred

Mountain. All three sat down to rest on a flat boulder near the top. They gazed in awe at the world below. Far in the distance they saw their village on the mesa above the ash, sycamore and cottonwood trees growing along the river. In other directions they saw different places, more rivers, and other mountains. As Quiet Water looked down into the crater at their camp in the meadow he felt as if he was flying above the earth. The boys waited all day to see the eagle fly, but they climbed down in disappointment.

In their haste to climb the mountain, and because darkness still prevailed as they left their camp, they had left the last leg of the antelope on a rock near the fire. When they returned from their day of waiting on the summit, the meat was gone.

"Look at these cougar tracks next to the rock," Screaming Crow said. "I'll hunt for more meat, but we must be careful during the night because the cougar may return for another meal."

Without waiting for an answer from his friends, Screaming Crow picked up his bow and arrows and disappeared among the aspen. Running Fox went out to gather more firewood, and Quiet Water walked to the spring with his weapons. Just as he heard the gurgling water, he saw a deer walking toward the spring. He lowered himself slowly and quietly onto the trail, and crept on his hands and knees, all the time hidden from the deer by the grasses and flowers of the meadow.

The deer lowered its head to drink from the spring as it stood in the midst of the carpet of reddish-pink flowers by the rocks. Quiet Water stopped, slipped the notch of an arrow around the bowstring, and pulled it back as far as he could. He aimed carefully, and just as the deer lifted its head from drinking and turned to leave, the arrow flew straight and true to the target.

Quiet Water called out to Screaming Crow to come to the spring so that he would know that there was enough meat for the camp, and no need to hunt further. A few minutes later, both Screaming Crow and Running Fox arrived at the spring to help carry the deer to camp.

After their evening meal, the boys hung the deer carcass high up in an aspen sapling to keep it away from cougars and bears. That night as Quiet Water kept watch, he heard a cougar growl nearby. He turned toward the sound, and tossed more wood on the fire.

Suddenly he saw the firelight bounce off two yellow eyes. The cougar stood near the tree from which the carcass hung. It growled slowly. Without taking his eyes away from the cougar's, Quiet Water stepped over to where his companions slept and shook their feet. "Wake up," he whispered. "Cougar."

Running Fox and Screaming Crow woke quickly and followed Quiet Water to the fire. The cougar was still nearby, watching them, its yellow eyes reflecting in the firelight. "If we throw a burning log toward the cougar, maybe it'll be frightened and leave us alone," Screaming Crow said.

"It smells the deer carcass," Running Fox said. "It won't be frightened for long."

"I would rather give the deer to the cougar than ask for a fight," Quiet Water said. "It's too dark to take a chance with our arrows."

"I think the best we can do is try to scare it away," Running Fox said. "I'll bet a flaming branch will make him think twice about coming any closer to our camp."

"Until he remembers the fresh meat again," Screaming Crow said.

The yellow eyes disappeared. The cougar growled

again, and then they heard the large lion leaping at the deer carcass. Running Fox reached for a burning branch from the fire and threw it toward the tree. The big cat yowled and crashed through the aspen grove to escape from the firebrand.

Screaming Crow tended the fire while the other two tried to sleep. The cougar's low growl in the distance made him keep the fire burning brightly. He had an arrow ready in his bow in case the cougar decided to return.

Running Fox kept his vigil the same way. The cougar's slow and guttural growl persisted until the first morning light.

Before waking the others, Running Fox walked to the aspen sapling that held the deer. Claw marks gouged the bark below the hanging carcass. Running Fox lowered it and sliced off enough meat for their morning meal, then hoisted it out of the cat's reach again. He laid the meat on the coals and woke his friends.

After finishing the tasty venison, they prepared for the morning's climb. Running Fox suggested they take a short cut he had noticed. "It is a steeper climb," he said. "But the distance is shorter if we go by way of the rock overhang."

Quiet Water and Screaming Crow voiced no objection to the idea. They gathered their bows and arrows and started toward the steep slope leading to the peak of the Sacred Mountain. The loose rocks along the route made the climb difficult. Their progress toward the summit slowed. "Once we pass the rock overhang, the footing should be better," Running Fox said.

"That's if we ever reach the overhang without sliding back down to the meadow," Screaming Crow said.

"We'll be bare-footed by the time we reach the top," Quiet Water said. "These rocks are sharp, and we will probably spend all day tomorrow patching our moccasins."

They had nearly reached the rock overhang when a female cougar came out of a dark entrance, inspected the intruders, and growled fiercely. The three climbers stopped short, and looked at their challenger, all quickly notching arrows on their bowstrings. "It's a female," Screaming Crow whispered. "By the look of her belly, she's nursing cubs."

"She is probably our visitor from last night," Quiet Water said. He touched the special arrow in its quiver.

"If she turns toward us," Running Fox said, "I can put an arrow through her heart."

"She will stay where she is unless we go closer," Screaming Crow said. "We should go back, and climb the ridge again. I don't want to take a chance on making her come for us. She's big and fast and she'll be hard to stop with our arrows. She will defend her cubs, and we could end up being her food."

"If we go back down we might miss watching the eagle fly," Running Fox said.

"The eagle will fly when the eagle wants to fly," Quiet Water said. "The sooner we leave the mother cougar alone with her cubs, the better."

Quiet Water had been following his friends along the trail. He turned and began the descent over the loose rocks. The other two backed down as the female cougar stood her ground, sounding her guttural growl in front of her den.

9

C H A P T E R
N I N E

THE SUN WARMED the meadow by the time the boys returned to camp. They decided to forego climbing to the summit that day and set to work cutting new soles from the deer hide for their worn-out moccasins.

They cut the new soles wider than the old ones. Running Fox sharpened one of the short spike antlers from the deer. When the soles were ready, Quiet Water soaked the soles and the thongs in the spring. Each took his turn using the sharpened antler to make holes along the edges of the new soles. Then, with their feet inside the moccasins, they inserted the thongs through the holes, and tied them across the top, attaching the new soles as best they could to continue their climbs to the summit of the Sacred Mountain.

They kept their feet in the moccasins until the hide had dried and shrunk to fit. To test their handiwork, they decided to walk around for the remaining part of the day.

The three clan brothers explored other parts of the crater, searching for berries, watching the wildlife, and looking at the many different flowers that were growing in the high meadow of the mountain.

They discovered another spring at the base of the second-highest peak. The flow of water from the rocky ground was less than from the spring near their camp, but the water was just as clear and cold, quenching their thirst. Below the spring, a stand of strawberry plants clustered around the water that trickled down into the meadow. A few of the strawberries were ripe, but most were still green. There were also many white blooms on the plants, promising more berries as the summer advanced.

They stooped to pick some of the ripe ones, and didn't see the huge, cinnamon-colored she-bear swaying toward the spring and the berry patch from an aspen grove. The bear saw the boys first, and stood up on its hind legs looking at them, wiggling her nose at their scent. The boys were taken by surprise when the bear gave a snort. It was as if she was telling them to leave.

Running Fox had an arrow on his bowstring ready to shoot.

"Wait!" Screaming Crow hissed.

Startled by Screaming Crow, Running Fox loosed his shot, and his arrow struck the bear in the shoulder. The bear roared with pain and snapped at the arrow, breaking the shaft with her jaws, then turned and dropped to all fours. She charged toward the boys. Momentarily paralyzed with fear, they stood together, staring at the advancing bear. They turned, terrified, and ran from her. Running Fox tripped over a clump of grass, and fell face-first onto the grassy floor of the meadow.

Quiet Water and Screaming Crow stopped and stared back at Running Fox. Beyond him, the bear lumbered across the meadow toward them. Screaming Crow ran back to help Running Fox as the bear closed in. Just as

Screaming Crow grabbed Running Fox and yanked him to his feet, the bear stopped ten paces away and stood on her hind legs. Her roar echoed against the rocky ridge and across the meadow.

Their eyes bulging in fear, the two boys huddled together. Screaming Crow pulled his knife from his belt with a trembling hand as the bear advanced with her front paws reaching out to grab them.

Quiet Water stood where Screaming Crow left him, his lower jaw slack with fear. Suddenly he knew what he had to do. He pulled the special arrow from the small quiver and quickly notched it onto his bowstring. Snapping and snarling and swinging her claws at them, the bear approached Running Fox and Screaming Crow as the boys stumbled backward away from her. Together, they tripped and fell backward over a small log. The bear stood over them, her eyes glistening with rage as she let out another deafening roar.

Quiet Water pulled the bowstring back as far as he could, aimed at the bear's heart, and released the special arrow. The eagle feathers guided the white-tipped arrow deep into the bear's heart. Quiet Water pulled his knife from his belt, and cautiously approached the bear. With a last anguished roar, the bear fell over backwards. Quiet Water stopped and waited until her legs stopped twitching.

Screaming Crow and Running Fox scrambled to their feet. The shaft of the special arrow protruded from the chest of the bear that had almost killed them.

"You saved our lives, Quiet Water," Running Fox said, still trembling.

"I was sure that bear had us when we fell," Screaming Crow added. "You shot her just in time."

"It was the special arrow that saved our lives," Quiet Water said, shoving his knife back into his belt as he stepped over to the huge, hairy carcass. He reached down and pulled the arrow from the bear's chest. As he held the shaft in his hands, he gazed in wonder at the bloody tip.

"Tall Deer once told me that the only way to hunt bear was with a pit-fall, not with a bow and arrows. We made a pit-fall once under a bee-tree down by the river. He showed me how to dig the hole in the ground, set the sharp stakes, and cover it all with willow saplings, dirt, and leaves."

"Everyone knows that it takes more than a bow and

arrow to kill a bear," Screaming Crow said. "I am still surprised this bear is no longer alive and charging us."

"That is because this is a special arrow," Quiet Water said softly, and walked to the spring to clean the bear's blood from the shaft and tip.

The bear's hide was tough. The three clan brothers were tired when they finished skinning. Running Fox carried several strips of meat. Screaming Crow and Quiet Water hoisted the heavy, rolled-up hide to their shoulders to carry it back to their camp.

As they made their way through the meadow, Quiet Water spoke to Running Fox. "How will your pretty girl from the Bear Clan feel after she learns that you killed a bear?"

"You killed the bear, I didn't."

"Perhaps your pretty girl will not believe you."

"You and Screaming Crow can tell her that I didn't kill the bear."

"We might decide not to tell her anything."

"You two are my clan brothers," Running Fox said, nervously.

Screaming Crow enjoyed listening to Running Fox worry. "That pretty girl from the Bear Clan might decide to go to the dances with Quiet Water and me. Besides, you are too short for such a pretty girl."

"From the way you speak about her, she must be very pretty," Quiet Water jibed.

Running Fox finally realized that his companions were joking.

"I think you both would give anything just to hold hands with my pretty girl from the Bear Clan."

"I think I like her sister better," Screaming Crow said.

10

THE THREE BOYS returned to their camp as the sun slipped slowly behind the rim of the ancient crater. The camp had not been disturbed. The deer carcass still hung from the aspen sapling, and there were enough coals to get the fire going again. They put the bear hide next to the lean-to.

"That cougar is sure to come back tonight to make another try at our venison," Running Fox said. "With those cubs to feed she will want some easy pickings."

"She will probably find the bear's carcass in the meadow," Screaming Crow remarked.

"It might be wise to cut off a quarter, and hang it where she can get it easily," Quiet Water said.

"I don't believe in giving a cougar meat I hunted," Running Fox said.

"Look at it this way," Screaming Crow replied. "If the cougar doesn't find the bear and comes here to our camp, we should give her some of our venison. She will fill her hunger easily, and leave us alone. I see nothing wrong with sharing with her. The Sacred Mountain is her home, not ours. We are intruders coming to watch the eagle fly."

"There is also plenty of game here for us," Quiet Water added. "I think Screaming Crow speaks well."

They separated a quarter of the venison and hung it on a sapling where the cougar could easily reach it. They packed the remainder in their hunting bags.

During Screaming Crow's turn to guard the camp, he heard the cougar growl. He had his bow ready with an arrow, but the growling stopped suddenly. The next noise that came to his ears was the cougar dragging the venison through the sparse undergrowth of the aspen grove. The next morning, they walked to the sapling. The meat was gone.

That day and the next brought the same disappointment. As they made their way down the ridge after the third day. Screaming Crow found an eagle feather on the branch of one of the young trees with blue-tinged needles growing near the base of the peak. He showed it to Quiet Water and Running Fox. The three sat by the campfire after a meal of roasted venison.

"For three days we have climbed to the top of the Sacred Mountain," Running Fox said. "For three days we have sat in silence waiting for the eagle to arrive. For three days we have returned to our camp with our bodies tired and our eyes hungry for the sight of the eagle. Today we are lucky. Screaming Crow has found an eagle feather. We need not climb to the summit again, feeling our legs ache and our lungs burn. We can return to the village with this eagle feather and no one will know that we didn't see the eagle fly."

The other two listened to Running Fox and for a long time sat in silence, thinking. Quiet Water looked at the eagle feather lying on the ground beside Screaming Crow. It was true that no one in the village would know that they had not seen the eagle fly. It might be that they could climb the peak for many days before the eagle decided to make an appearance. He also thought that the eagle might fly around the peak as they watched, and never drop a feather from its plumage for them to bring home to the old medicine man.

Quiet Water also recalled the words of Swift Elk expressing the fears of the elders that he will someday leave the village with the secrets of the Eagle Clan. He thought about trying to find his parents in California and becoming John Butler again. He yearned to find a place where there was no one who feared that he would betray his clan brothers. Yet, if they returned without seeing the eagle fly, they would never know the greatest secret of the clan. John Butler—Quiet Water—John Butler—Quiet Water . . .

His thoughts turned to his life in the village on top of the mesa with Tall Deer and Blue-Flower-Blooming. Tall Deer had spoken up for him in the presence of the doubting elders of the Eagle Clan. Blue-Flower-Blooming loved him as if he was her own child. How sad they would be if he left the village. He felt the weight of the silver bracelet on his wrist. The fletching of the special arrow glowed in the firelight. It would be terrible to lose again all that he had grown to love.

Suddenly, the face of Swift Elk appeared in the smoke rising from the dying fire. In the eyes of the old medicine man, Quiet Water saw again the magic he had seen when Swift Elk told them about climbing the Sacred Mountain to watch the eagle fly. There must be something important to learn from watching the eagle fly.

The campfire was a bed of red coals when Quiet Water finally broke the silence. "Running Fox, Screaming Crow," He began. "You are my brothers and best friends. We have grown up together, learned to hunt together, and we have eaten our food together. We have shared our lives."

Quiet Water held the feather between his fingers. "I would like to return to our village with this eagle feather that Screaming Crow has found. My body is tired from the climbing and my eyes are sore and empty from searching the sky. When Swift Elk told us about the Sacred Mountain, and how we must wait to see the eagle fly, I did not know anything. Now, I can see how his old, clouded eyes flashed like pine needles in a fire as he talked about watching the eagle. I cannot forget the look in Swift Elk's eyes. All I know is we must continue climbing and waiting until the eagle decides we are ready to watch it fly. "

The three sat in silence in front of the campfire's red

coals. Finally, Running Fox took the eagle feather from Quiet Water and placed it on the coals of the fire. The three young clan brothers watched the feather burst into flame and quickly turn to ashes.

II

CHAPTER
ELEVEN

STORM CLOUDS covered the top of the mountain in the morning, but the boys climbed the familiar ridge. By early afternoon, the rain began splattering against the boulders, thunder boomed and echoed, and lightning streaked earthward, charging the air with electricity, making the hair on their heads stand straight out from their scalps. They scurried down from the peak and were glad to reach their camp in the meadow.

The storm rolled in the following morning, but by early afternoon the sun broke through the scattering clouds. The boys reached the top of the peak just as the storm drifted away. The thin mountain air smelled fresh. The boulders looked scrubbed, and the tiny, delicate flowers seemed to dance in the gentle breeze. They took their places on the boulder to search the sky for the eagle.

Screaming Crow suddenly rose to his feet, putting his hands to his brow to shade his eyes from the sun. High above the mountain he saw a black speck disappear into a cloud. The others turned to look in the same direction. As they strained their eyes to discover what Screaming Crow had seen, it appeared at the other end of the cloud. The boys remained silent, watching as it circled the Sacred Mountain, growing larger as it soared nearer and nearer.

An eagle suddenly took shape as it flew a wide circle, approaching the summit. There was no need for words. The boys felt themselves tingling, and their hearts beat quickly with excitement as the beautiful

bird, with its broad wing span, swooped down to inspect them. It veered off the peak, and continued its downward flight, just clearing the forest canopy below. They followed the eagle's flight until it disappeared into a canyon. They kept their eyes focused on the canyon.

The boys were startled by a loud, screeching cry coming from behind them. They turned quickly to see the eagle gliding gracefully on the wind. It had left the canyon, circled the mountain, and surprised them. It called them to witness the joy of flight and freedom as it soared, circled, climbed, and dove, using its large wings on the wind. The three stood speechless at the perfect balance of the eagle, the wind, and the Sacred Mountain.

Finally, the eagle climbed until it disappeared into the sky again. Thinking the eagle had decided to leave, the dejected boys began to climb down from the summit. Before they had climbed down fifty yards, the eagle began a wide, plunging circle toward the top of the peak. With its talons outstretched, and its broad wings braking against the wind, it made a perfect landing on the large boulder where the boys had spent so many hours waiting.

The three eagle watchers braced themselves against the steep slope as they witnessed the eagle's return. Running Fox started back up the ridge, and as he approached the top, the eagle spread its wings for take-off. As the huge bird became airborne, a single feather fluttered to the ground in front of Running Fox. He picked up the feather and held it high for his clan brothers to see. Smiling and exhilarated, the boys walked down the ridge while the eagle disappeared into the sunset.

The next morning, the three young men made preparations to return to the village. They untied the thongs that held the frame together and dismantled the lean-to. Screaming Crow put the thongs from the antelope hide in his hunting bag. They put the thatching and poles on the fire to burn so that their footsteps would be the only trace of their visit to the Sacred Mountain.

They finished the last of the venison that morning. "We should hunt for another deer to have food for our journey home," Running Fox said.

"It would be better to wait until we are off the steep slopes before we load ourselves with the weight of a deer," Screaming Crow replied. "We'll pass where the fire burned, and hunt for another antelope."

"What if the antelope are not there?" Running Fox asked. "We have a long journey home."

"We will find something to hunt, somewhere," Screaming Crow said, and looked up at the sky full of white billowing thunderheads. "Let's get down before the clouds gather together for another storm."

Running Fox held up the eagle feather. "I think Quiet Water should have the honor of carrying the eagle feather to Swift Elk," he said. "If it was not for your patience and loyalty, I would have settled for the feather Screaming Crow found." Screaming Crow took the feather and spun it slowly between his fingers. He looked at the pale blue sky, then handed the feather to Quiet Water.

Solemnly, Quiet Water took the feather, and they left the meadow. It was a happy journey for the three clan brothers, especially for Quiet Water, who no longer pondered his life as John Butler, nor worried about the doubting elders. If they continued their doubt, they would be doubting for nothing. He looked fondly at the silver bracelet his father, Tall Deer, had given him, and knew he would no longer need to sit on the ledge when he returned.

The steep downward slopes slowed their progress.

They stopped occasionally to watch a pair of blue-jays call to each other, and a squirrel with long ears and a bushy tail climb a tree trying to hide from them. They left the trees with blue needles behind, and wove their way through giant fir that finally gave way to the red-orange-barked ponderosa pine.

Quiet Water stopped suddenly, turned, and motioned to the others to remain still. He stepped behind a nearby pine whose trunk was wide enough to keep him hidden as he got an arrow notched in his bowstring. The other two stood motionless, watching their companion without knowing what he was doing. Quiet Water slowly eased himself into shooting position, pulling the bowstring back as far as he could, aiming high to the top of a tall ponderosa pine. He released the bowstring, and the arrow flew quickly upward. They heard the loud sound of flapping wings as several turkeys launched themselves into hurried flight, and then a *thump* as a large male turkey hit the ground under the tree in front of Quiet Water. The arrow had gone clear through the big bird, taking the turkey's life before it fell to the forest floor.

Quiet Water went quickly to his prize. "That was a

great shot," Screaming Crow said, walking over to join Quiet Water. "Turkeys are very difficult to hunt, especially when they're high in a tree."

"With all the tree branches up there, how did you find a clean shot?" Running Fox asked.

"This bird was the only one I had a shot at," Quiet Water said. "The others were blocked by branches. This is the one that was moving and caught my eye at first. I had doubts that I would hit him, but I tried anyway."

"We are almost down the steep slopes. A turkey is not as heavy as a deer to carry," Running Fox said. "You were right about waiting to hunt, Screaming Crow."

"You two gather the wood," Screaming Crow said. "I will prepare the turkey." Running Fox and Quiet Water looked at each other and smiled.

Screaming Crow quickly pulled the feathers from the turkey, and cleaned out the offal, saving the heart, liver, and gizzard to bake with the meat. He built a fire near a stream. Next to the fire, Screaming Crow dug a hole large enough to hold the turkey and coals from the fire. While they waited for the fire to burn down into red hot coals, Screaming Crow took the bird to the stream and plastered it with a thick layer of mud.

As they relaxed by the fire, the three divided the turkey feathers among themselves to use for arrows and decorations.

Quiet Water thought about his life with his friends in the village compared to what he remembered about the neighbors he had in Tennessee. In Tennessee everybody seemed to compete against one another constantly. If it wasn't getting the corn or hay harvested first, it was winning foot races or selling cattle for a higher price than a neighbor.

Here, with the Eagle Clan, there wasn't that competition. There was friendly joking like when they first camped by the waterfall, and he and Running Fox had killed the rabbits. Running Fox had said that Screaming Crow could have the tails to eat. Of course, all three shared the meat just as they had shared everything on the journey to the Sacred Mountain.

But he also remembered when their neighbors in Tennessee lost their barn to a fire. Everyone for miles around had gone to help build a new barn. It was just different with the clan. There was no ceremony to sharing, and competition was something to joke about, but never take seriously.

The fire burned down into red-hot coals. Screaming Crow took a flat rock and pushed half the coals into the hole. Quiet Water and Running Fox lifted the mud-plastered turkey and placed it on the glowing coals and Screaming Crow scraped the remaining coals from the fire on top to cover the mud. Then the three went out through the forest to gather more firewood for the night while they waited for the turkey to bake in its mud shell.

"I think I will miss climbing the Sacred Mountain to watch for the eagle," Running Fox said as they sat waiting for their meal to cook in the coals.

Quiet Water and Screaming Crow agreed that they too would miss the adventure. "It is something we will always remember," Screaming Crow said.

Quiet Water said. "Longing for what is lost can be painful to the heart. This memory of watching the eagle fly fills my heart with joy. I used to miss my other parents. For a long time, my heart cried out to me. Yet, when we were climbing the Sacred Mountain, I did not think about them. I thought about Tall Deer and Blue-Flower-Blooming. It was them I missed and I knew I would return to them at the end of this quest."

"I learned that my impatience is something I needed to shed like a rattlesnake sheds its skin," Running Fox said. "Now I will think about things before rushing to do anything."

"I thought I was a better hunter than everyone," Screaming Crow said. "And I used it as an excuse to get out of working to carry water to the corn, or to pull weeds. Now, I am proud of Quiet Water's great shot that brought us this turkey for our meal. I know that I'm needed in the fields as well as on a hunt. I'll no longer slip away from work."

Quiet Water poked at the hard, baked mud around the turkey with a sharpened willow stick from the stream bank. "The willow stick passes easily through the meat," he said. "It's time to eat."

"Good. I am hungry enough to eat the mud too," Screaming Crow said.

Using the willow stick, he and Quiet Water lifted the turkey, heavy with the baked mud, from the mound of dead coals. They removed the baked mud and saw that the meat was white and steaming, ready to enjoy. "It was your arrow that gave us this feast, Quiet Water," Screaming Crow said. "You should have the first choice."

"I will wait until the turkey cools," Quiet Water said, grinning at Screaming Crow. "A chunk of this meat may not burn fingers, but it will surely burn the tongue."

"But, we are hungry," Screaming Crow said. "We have to wait for you to choose. I'll starve. Besides, by that time, the turkey will be cold."

"You may choose first, Screaming Crow," Quiet Water replied. "Has some of Running Fox's impatience been transferred to you?"

Running Fox grabbed one of the turkey's legs, and tore it off with a twist. As he waved it back and forth to cool, he smiled at his companions. "It is not impatience that teaches me how to cool down the leg of the turkey, it is hunger," he said. "Take it, Quiet Water; it will not burn your tongue now."

"You are clever, Running Fox," Quiet Water said, enjoying the game. "You may eat first, because I do not choose a leg." Then he reached down to the turkey with his knife and cut a chunk of meat from the breast. "Now you two can burn your tongues if you want to."

12

C H A P T E R
T W E L V E

THE FIRST LIGHT of morning seeped through the forest of tall ponderosa pine. Screaming Crow heard the yipping of a family of coyotes in the distance. He stood up, and looked toward the sound. Four coyotes trotted in a line toward the camp. Screaming Crow stood perfectly still. The coyotes continued trotting toward him until the leader, a large female, stopped, lifted her nose upward, and sniffed. The three others stopped also, and began picking up the strange scent with their noses. The leader then lowered her head almost to the ground, and without taking her eyes away from the statue-like figure of Screaming Crow, began to sidestep back and forth. Then she backed up, still watching. The others sat motionless, watching Screaming Crow.

"Hoopa, Coyote friend," Screaming Crow said. "Come closer, and I will give you the bones of our turkey. Or are you too wise to trust such a gift?"

The large female cocked her head, listening to the strange sound of Screaming Crow's voice. He reached down and grabbed the picked-clean carcass of the turkey, and threw it as far as he could toward the coyotes. His movement startled the animals, and they raced away until the large female stopped to look back. Screaming Crow ducked behind a tree trunk, out of the coyotes' sight. As he peeked around the trunk, he watched the leader slink back, belly almost dragging on the brown, fallen pine needles, toward the turkey bones.

Screaming Crow smiled as he watched the coyote stop momentarily at the carcass, look around carefully, grab the bones with her teeth, and dart quickly back to the other three. They followed their leader as she disappeared into the forest.

Screaming Crow rousted the others from their sleep, and told them about the visit from the coyotes as they ate the cold turkey. Then they continued their journey back to their village.

They didn't stop for a swim in the pool under the

waterfall because all three were eager to return and report to Swift Elk and their families. But Quiet Water looked at the wide layer of clay in the stream-bank. "This is good clay. We should come back on our horses, dig this clay, and bring it back to our village. Our mothers can make their pottery from it."

"Dig a handful to take with us," Running Fox said. "If it is the kind of clay they like for their pottery, we can come back with extra horses to carry a lot back to them."

Quiet Water dug out a little of the clay, wrapped it in a piece of the antelope hide, and put it in his hunting bag. He hoped Blue-Flower-Blooming would like the clay for her pottery. He wanted to be able to return for a good-sized load to contribute to her efforts.

As they walked up the trail to the mesa, they agreed to meet on their horses by the river after listening to Swift Elk and returning to their houses. "I will ride by the house of the pretty girl from the Bear Clan," Running Fox said.

"We will ride with you," Quiet Water said. "Perhaps there is more than one pretty girl from the Bear Clan, one who would like to ride on White Star."

"And, I want to see her sister," Screaming Crow said.

Quiet Water looked forward to seeing the mouse-colored mare with her colt and feeling her power as they loped along the river's edge. He also wondered what it would be like to become acquainted with a pretty girl from the Bear Clan.

When they arrived at the village of stone houses on top of the mesa, they went directly to Swift Elk. Quiet Water handed the old medicine man the eagle feather. Swift Elk looked at the feather in his hand, and his cloudy eyes brightened once again.

"As I once did many summers ago, you have seen the eagle fly. It was an experience I have never forgotten. You have seen the eagle's graceful flight and witnessed its joy in being as free as the wind it masters. You have seen the Sacred Mountain with your young eyes. You have seen a perfect mountain with perfect beings in perfect balance. You will keep this experience with you always, and when your eyes are cloudy and dull as mine are, you will still remember the Sacred Mountain while you are waiting for your sons to return from their own quests for the eagle feather."

He turned toward Quiet Water. "It is you who hands

me the gift of the eagle feather. I know that in some way you earned that honor from your clan brothers. What you have done and what you have seen is between the three of you only to remember, even as your lives fade with time."

Quiet Water, Running Fox, and Screaming Crow returned to their houses. Tall Deer and Blue-Flower-Blooming smiled warmly as their son approached. Quiet Water had been smiling since he left Swift Elk.

"We are happy that you have returned safely from the Sacred Mountain," Tall Deer said, his arms outstretched for a welcoming embrace.

"I am more than happy to be back with you," Quiet Water said, smiling.

Tears of joy slipped from Blue-Flower-Blooming's eyes as she held Quiet Water closely to her. Quiet Water held out the special arrow in its quiver to Tall Deer. "Why are you giving this to me?" Tall Deer asked.

"It is yours," said Quiet Water. "I used it to kill a bear."

"You must share your story with us tonight, so that all may hear. The special arrow is yours now, until you have a son who will carry it to the Sacred Mountain to watch the eagle fly. In time, your son will give it to his son, and so on, forever." Tears rolled down his cheeks.

Quiet Water put his arms around Tall Deer and Blue-Flower-Blooming. "Thank you, Father and Mother. The eagle showed me where I belong. I belong here with the Eagle Clan. You, father and mother, are my family."

ABOUT THE AUTHOR

JOHN DUNCKLEE found his inspiration for *Quest for the Eagle Feather* during his four years of work on "Man-Land Relationships on the San Francisco Peaks"; an environmental impact statement, published in 1973, that was influential in saving "the Sacred Mountain" from a real estate development on Hart Prairie. During the course of his research, John forged a number of wonderful friendships with the Hopi and Navajo people. John and his wife Penny divide their time between Oracle and Alpine, Arizona.

A preview of
another exciting title from

rising moon
Books for Young Readers from Northland Publishing

Danger in the Desert

by T. S. Fields

SEVEN

Robbie sat up with a start. "A snake! How'd we get a snake in here?"

No way was I going to sit and explain how I knew there was a snake in the car while it crawled around me somewhere in the dark. It might even be a rattler getting ready to strike. I squirmed, feeling for the door handle. No way I was staying in the car with a snake. "Just get out," I yelled to Robbie. "We gotta get out of the car now."

Both the front and back doors opened at the same time, and we jumped from the car. "Ow," yelled Robbie. "I think I stepped on something." He hobbled to the front of the car and examined the bottom of his sock in the glare of the headlights. "I don't see anything on my foot. I guess the ground was just hard. It wouldn't have hurt if I had my shoes on." Then he looked at me. "Why do you think there's a snake in the car? We've had the windows shut and the doors locked. Maybe you were just dreaming."

"Well, not exactly . . ."

"Yeah, well what exactly then?" Robbie looked part asleep, past confused, and part mad. "Well . . ."

"Well, I had to go to the bathroom."

"Yeah, and . . ."

"And well . . . I went to put on my shoes, so I could go out a little ways into the desert."

"I thought we were supposed to leave our shoes outside for them to get water. What'd you do with the water that was in your shoes?"

"I put it in yours."

"Oh, thanks a lot!"

"Robbie!" I shouted. There was silence in the desert night as the two of us glared at each other. But then I decided that maybe if I went over exactly how the snake got in the car, I could think how to get it out, so I said, "I got one shoe on, see," and I pointed to my foot to show him it wasn't just my imagination. "Then I went to put the other one on. Everything happened so fast from there, but I think when I bent down to pick up my other shoe from the ground, a little field mouse ran onto it. And then suddenly, I thought I saw this big snake coming at my shoe from under the car. Then part of it rose up off the ground and the whole thing slithered into the car real fast. That's when I screamed and told you to get out."

Robbie looked at me for a minute, and then he bit his lip. "Okay, if you think that's what happened, then I guess we better find out."

We decided to walk back to the car door and open it. That way the inside light would go on and then maybe we could at least see the snake. I put my hand on the door handle and took a deep breath. Everything had happened so fast with the mouse and my shoe that I wasn't sure if we'd see nothing, or if a big, poisonous snake would spring at us.

I opened the driver's car door and jumped back just in case the snake was ready to strike. Robbie stared through the passenger side window onto the now-lighted seat. "Holey moley, there's a big snake on our front seat."

"That's what I've been trying to tell you," I shouted, slamming the door shut again.

"I can't believe it," Robbie said over and over again.

"I told you it was there."

"Scott, we gotta do something. There's a snake sitting on the front seat of the car, and we're out here where there's probably a zillion other snakes just waiting to bite us or squeeze us or something." He looked sort of glassy-eyed. "What are we gonna do?"

I ran my hand through my hair. I didn't know what we were going to do. I didn't want to stay out here all night any more than Robbie did. There were lots of strange noises, and all we could see was the path lighted by the headlights. Who knew what was out here in the darkness just beyond the headlights?

"I've got an idea," Robbie said. "Why don't we turn the radio on real loud and leave the car door open? Maybe that will bother the snake's ears so much that it will crawl away from the music."

I looked at my little brother. "I don't think snakes have ears!"

"You got a better idea?"

There was a loud hooting sound in the distance and Robbie and I both jumped. "Okay, we'll try it," I said. I didn't think it would work, but I didn't have any better plan. We crept back to the car door and stared into the window, but without the interior light on, it was too hard to see anything. "So, uh, you want to open the door this time?" I said. After all, Robbie was always complaining that I took over just because I was older.

"Okay," he said. "And then you reach in and turn on the radio. And be really careful, because when we looked before, the snake was curled up on the seat right next to the radio."

"I dunno, Robbie. What if the snake is still right there. I don't think I could get my hand away if it started to strike."

Robbie sighed. "Maybe it isn't such a great plan."

Robbie and I looked at each other, each of us feeling fear and frustration. Finally, I said, "Why don't we at least open the car door and see where the snake is? Maybe it moved away from the radio."

Of course, we had no idea what to do if the snake was still right by the radio, but there didn't seem to be any other thing to do except open the car door and see where the snake was. I put my hand on the doorknob, took a deep breath, threw open the door and jumped back in case the snake was right there. Robbie jumped too, and we almost tripped over each other. No snake emerged from the car, and keeping the open door carefully in our sight at all times, we walked back toward the car. With the light on inside, it was plain to see that the snake hadn't moved. It was a big and it had black, whitish-yellow, and dark red on it. Robbie whispered, "Is that a rattler?"

"I don't think so," I whispered back; "but it could be. I don't want to find out. It doesn't look very friendly."

We decided it was just too dangerous to try for the radio, and besides, we didn't know if snakes really moved away from music or not. We climbed up on the hood of the car and sat down. That way we could stare through the front window at the snake and see if it crawled out. Meanwhile, we'd be off the ground in case the snake had any friends slithering around looking for it.

Robbie's and my eyes glared through the windshield at the snake. If eye power could have moved it, that snake would have been gone. Instead, it seemed perfectly content to be coiled up on the front seat of the car, and why not? The car seat was a lot more comfortable than the hard metal hood we were sitting on. I looked up at the sky. The stars were so bright. I could easily see both the big and the little dipper. I'd once read a book about a guy who used the stars to guide him, and I wished I could remember how he'd done it.

After a while, my rear hurt from sitting on the hood. Robbie said he was more tired than he'd ever been in his whole life, but he didn't plan to sleep until we could get back into a locked car. That worried me. I knew that we were going to have a really hard day tomorrow. We needed all our strength, and that meant we needed to sleep some tonight. But how to get the snake out and us into the car, I just didn't know. "What's that?" Robbie whispered.

There was a strange noise off to the right. "Probably nothing." I whispered back.

"What kind of nothing makes that kind of noise?"

"I don't know."

Robbie wrapped his arms around himself. "Scott, we gotta get back in the car. We really do."

I thought and thought until I thought my brain would burst. "Okay, I got it. We'll get the jack out of the car. Since it's strong enough to hold up the car, it ought to be strong enough to kill a snake, right?" I was beginning to feel my heart pump. Now this was a plan that could work.

"I'll take the jack, and I'll hit the snake. Then the snake will be dead, and I'll use the jack to push it out of the car." I raised an eyebrow. "Pretty good idea, huh?"

Robbie looked at me. "I think it's a great idea. Really. I think it was so smart of you to think of, but . . . Now, don't get mad or anything. I'm not saying this to be mean. But I think I should be the one to hit the snake."

"You?"

"Yeah, in baseball, you miss so much of the time. Scott,

we can't strike out when it comes to the snake."

I started to say something mean back to him, sort of reflex action, but I had to admit that he was right about whose aim was better. Robbie was the leading hitter on the baseball team; he was better than a lot of the older guys. Still, I thought I should be the one to take the risk with the snake. After all, I was the older brother. I went around to the back of the station wagon. I was pretty sure that when Robbie saw how heavy a jack was, he'd change his mind about who should use it.

We climbed over the roof of the car and leaned over the back of it. I grabbed the station wagon's back door handle. Swinging the door open, we peered upside down into the back of the car. "Uh, Robbie, you know where the jack is?"

"Nope, I don't think I've ever seen a jack except on TV when I saw guys fixing flat tires."

Truthfully, that was the only place I'd ever seen one, too. On TV they'd just opened the trunk of the car and there'd been a spare tire and a jack. The only problem with that was that a station wagon didn't have a trunk. Maybe a station wagon didn't have a spare tire or a jack, either. I began to get a sinking feeling, but I didn't give up. Much as I hated to, I climbed off the car. Standing on the ground, I stared again into the back of the station wagon. There was a third seat that could be pulled up out of storage space in the back, and I release the levers and pulled, hoping to see a jack. I looked in the wells in the back, but zip. Nothing. No jack.

I rubbed my eyes. Why couldn't anything go right? "Come on, Robbie, let's climb back on the hood of the car, and we'll try to think of something else." When we were sitting on the car and staring through the windshield, we could easily see the snake on the front seat. It was creepy looking. I looked at my hand and thought about how the thing moving across it had been that big snake, and I shuddered.

The headlights didn't seem as bright to me as they were before, and I began to worry that if we didn't think of something pretty soon, we were going to be sitting out here on the hood of the car in pitch black darkness. Staring ahead, I could see a small Palo Verde tree in the headlights. "Robbie," I said slowly, thinking as I spoke, "See that tree over there? I'm going to go get a branch off of it, and we'll use the branch to push the snake out of the car.

"Okay," Robbie said wearily.

I had only one shoe on. My other foot was barefoot. I had been walking around the car very carefully, but the Joshua tree was a ways away. I couldn't risk getting cactus stickers in my foot, so I decided I would have to hop to the Palo Verde tree. I was really sorry that I'd ever taken off my basketball shoes in the first place. It was a dumb idea. By tomorrow, whatever water they'd gathered would probably have soaked into the shoes anyway.

As I got a little ways away from the car, the sounds of the desert seemed even more threatening. I made myself keep hopping because I knew that if I really stopped to listen, I'd run right back to the car. Finally, I'd hopped to the Joshua tree. It was a scraggly little thing, and the branches were pretty puny. I wished I'd had my Boy Scout knife to cut one off, but it was sitting at home next to my bed on my nightstand. I leaned down and cleared a spot so that I could put both feet down. It felt great to stand on two feet, but I worried a lot about my bare foot. I knew there were scorpions and all kinds of other yucky bugs out here, and I hoped my bare foot wouldn't make a tempting target.

I found the smallest long branch on the tree, and I began to twist it back and forth, then up and down. I was panting with effort, and the dumb branch still clung to the tree. The next thing I knew something was coming up behind me. I jumped around, screamed, and made a fist. I might only have one punch, but whatever it was, I'd give it my best shot before it attacked.

"Don't hit . . . It's me. It's just me!" Robbie yelled.

My heart was pounding a million miles an hour. "What . . . what are you doing here?" I gasped. "You scared me to death!"

"Sorry. While I was sitting on the hood, I saw something gleaming from the road. I got off the car to see what it was, and guess what . . . it was a tin can. I took my shoes, poured the water from my shoes into the can, and look, I'm here! Of course, my shoes are a gross mess, but at least I have 'em on, and we still have the water." Robbie looked proud of himself. I was proud of him too, and I told him so. Maybe I didn't give my little brother enough credit.

Together, we worked on the tree branch. It certainly didn't want to leave that tree. Finally, we got it free, and we headed back to the car. I held on to Robbie's shoulder as I hopped my way back. When we reached the car, we approached the open door very carefully. A first glance told us that the snake wasn't still on the seat, and almost in unison, Robbie and I looked down at our feet to make sure nothing was slithering toward us. Then we noticed the snake. It was still in the car; it had just moved to the floor.

"Exactly how are we gonna do this?" Robbie whispered. "That branch isn't very heavy. If we hit the snake with it, he might just get mad instead of dead."

I looked at the snake. It couldn't possibly have grown since we'd been out getting the branch. It must have just spread out a little more. I gulped. "I guess we're just going to have to use the stick to shove him out." My throat felt real dry. My hands were shaking so much that I held the branch with both hands. "Go around and open the other door, then come back over here. We'll stand here behind him, and we'll shove him out the driver's side door. I leaned into the car on the passenger side, and I noticed that the beige part of the snake almost blended in with the beige carpet on the floor. I heard Robbie take a sharp breath, and then I heard a ringing in my ears as I edged the branch closer and closer to the snake. I felt like I might pass out. The ringing got louder, and then I felt the stick touch the snake. It took all the willpower I had not to scream and pull the stick away. Instead, I made myself put the stick next to the middle of the snake, and then I pushed as hard as I could toward the open door. There was a hissing sound.

OTHER BOOKS FROM RISING MOON

Danger in the Desert, by T. S. Fields
Walks in Beauty, by Hazel Krantz

AVAILABLE IN THE FALL OF 1997:
The Last Warrior, by Suzanne Pierson Ellison
Tending the Fire: The Story of Maria Martinez, by Juddi Morris
Whichaway, by Glendon and Kathryn Swarthout

AVAILABLE IN THE SPRING OF 1998:
Lolo and Red-Legs, by Kirk Reeve
Twilight Boy, by Timothy Green
Where Black Bears Roar, by Ruth M. Covault

OTHER BOOKS FROM JOHN DUNCKLEE

Good Year for the Buzzards, University of Arizona Press, 1994
Coyotes I Have Known, University of Arizona Press, 1996